D0266296

South Dublin Libraries
www.southdublinlibraries.ie

First published in the UK in 2018
by New Frontier Publishing Europe Ltd
93 Harbord Street, London SW6 6PN
www.newfrontierpublishing.co.uk

Originally published in China by
Zhejiang Juvenile and Children's Publishing House.

ISBN: 978-1-912076-74-1 (HB)

Text and Illustrations copyright © Fu Wenzheng 2017
The rights of Fu Wenzheng to be identified as the author and illustrator of this
work have been asserted.

All rights reserved.

This book is sold subject to the condition that it shall not, by way of trade or
otherwise, be lent, hired out or otherwise circulated in any form of binding or
cover other than that in which it is published. No part of this publication may be
reproduced, stored in a retrieval system, or transmitted in any form or by any means
(electronic, mechanical, photocopying, recording or otherwise) without the prior
written permission of New Frontier Publishing Europe Ltd.

A CIP catalogue record for this book is available from
the British Library.

Printed in China
10 9 8 7 6 5 4 3 2 1

Ash
dresses her friends

South Dublin Libraries
www.southdublinlibraries.ie

Fu Wenzheng

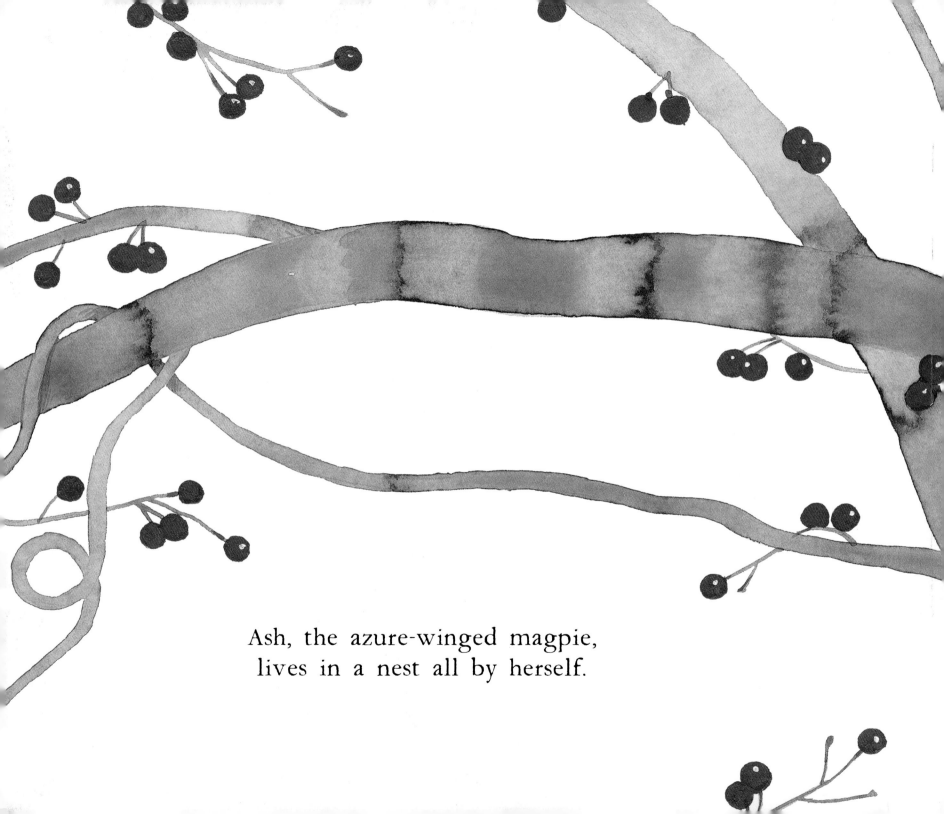

Ash, the azure-winged magpie,
lives in a nest all by herself.

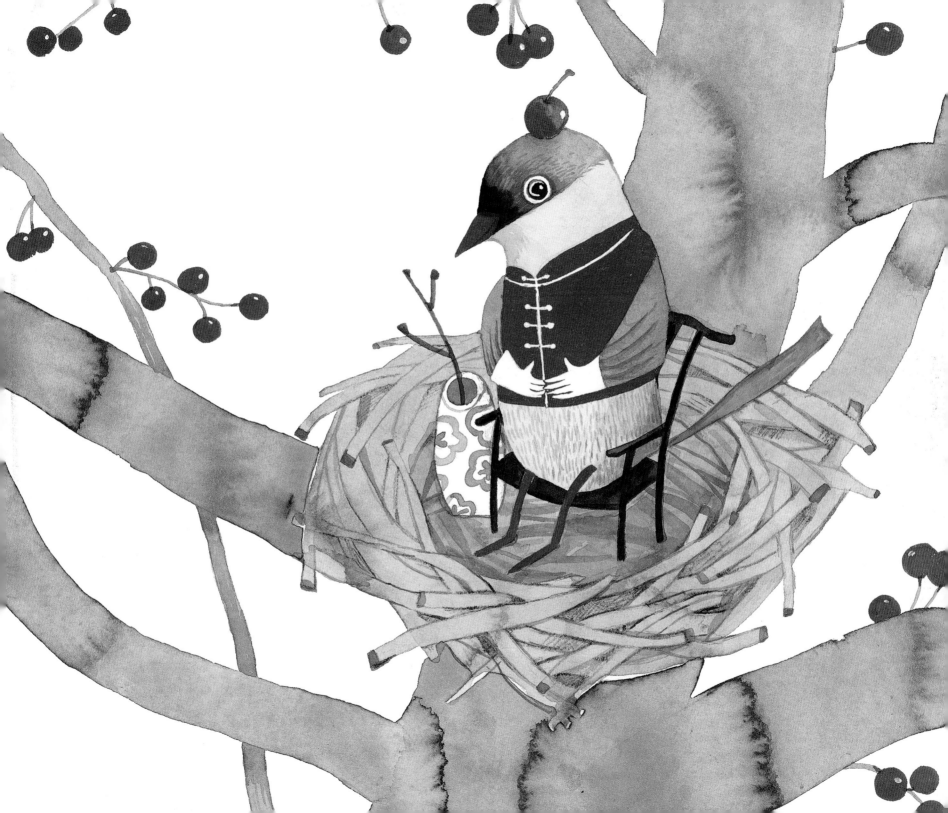

Whenever her neighbours have
a party, Ash is very quiet.
No-one speaks to her.
They all think Ash is shy.

Ash sits on her own.

She wishes she had someone
to play with.

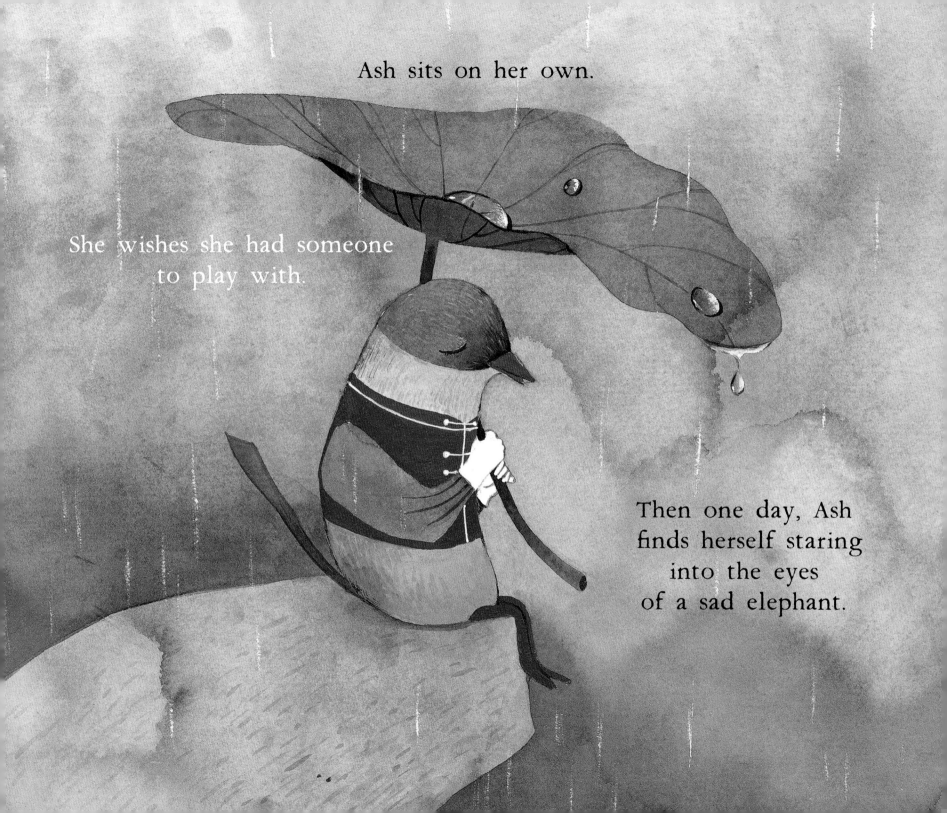

Then one day, Ash
finds herself staring
into the eyes
of a sad elephant.

'I really want a new shirt,' says the elephant.

'Why are you sighing?' Ash asks.

'I can help you!' Ash smiles.

The next morning, Ash appears
holding some beautiful red patterned material.

She sings while she makes a
shirt for the elephant.

South Dublin Libraries

www.southdublinlibraries.ie

The elephant is so happy. He tells all the other animals about Ash ...

... and the red patterned material.

'Can you make me a new dress?'
a timid black bear asks
nervously.

Ash sets to work.

The black bear begins to dance in her new dress. But there is still so much material left.

'I'm covered in
black-and-white stripes.
I need a bit of colour!
Ash, could you help
me?' the zebra asks.

Ash makes a cover for
the zebra's armchair
out of the red patterned
material.

Ash looks at all the material she still has left.

She makes a scarf
for the fox ...

... and a backpack for the koala.
Koala's baby sleeps soundly in the red patterned backpack.

South Dublin Libraries

www.southdublinlibraries.ie

Ash makes a patterned bag for the
grey squirrel.
He uses it to gather pine cones.

There is not much material left now:

just enough to make a
quilt for the little snail.

Now all the patterned cloth is gone

and so are all Ash's friends.

Then the squirrel arrives
with his bag.

'Thanks, Ash! All my friends
like my beautiful bag!'

He shows Ash the pine cones
he has collected in it.

All Ash's friends visit her to celebrate the things she has made.

They feel very loved and so does Ash.